MW00902886

ARE YOU SURE THAT WAS A RABBIT?
BY CLAY HARPER & JAS INGRAM

Other Schiffer Books on Related Subjects:
Boomer Explores Annapolis, 978-0-7643-4008-6, $12.99
Busy Bodies: Play Like the Animals, 978-0-7643-3832-8, $14.99
Ronnie Raven Recycles, 978-0-7643-3840-3, $16.99

Library of Congress Control Number: 2011942740

Type set in Comic Sans

ISBN: 978-0-7643-4007-9
Printed in China

Schiffer Books are available at special discounts for bulk purchases for sales promotions or premiums. Special editions, including personalized covers, corporate imprints, and excerpts can be created in large quantities for special needs. For more information contact the publisher:

Published by Schiffer Publishing Ltd.
4880 Lower Valley Road
Atglen, PA 19310
Phone: (610) 593-1777; Fax: (610) 593-2002
E-mail: Info@schifferbooks.com

For the largest selection of fine reference books on this and related subjects, please visit our website at **www.schifferbooks.com**
We are always looking for people to write books on new and related subjects. If you have an idea for a book, please contact us at proposals@schifferbooks.com

This book may be purchased from the publisher.
Include $5.00 for shipping.
Please try your bookstore first.
You may write for a free catalog.

In Europe, Schiffer books are distributed by
Bushwood Books
6 Marksbury Ave.
Kew Gardens
Surrey TW9 4JF England
Phone: 44 (0) 20 8392 8585; Fax: 44 (0) 20 8392 9876
E-mail: info@bushwoodbooks.co.uk
Website: www.bushwoodbooks.co.uk

ARE YOU SURE THAT WAS A RABBIT?

BY CLAY HARPER & JAS INGRAM

IT WAS A **BEAUTIFUL DAY**
SO MS. GWINN DECIDED TO TAKE OUR CLASS
OUTSIDE FOR A NATURE WALK.

BUT FIRST...

we STRETCHED.

WE DID YOGA...

WE SANG LOVELY DAY...

WE LINED UP
WITH ALL EYES FORWARD
AND FINALLY...

WE WERE READY TO GO

WE WALKED TO THE
ORGANIC GARDEN.

AN ORGANIC GARDEN
IS A PLACE WHERE VEGETABLES
ARE GROWN WITHOUT CHEMICALS.
IN OUR GARDEN EVERYBODY HELPS.
WE GROW LETTUCE,
TOMATOES, GARLIC, RADISHES,
MELONS AND MORE.

MS. GWINN!

Hardly.

THAT WASN'T A RAT RASHEE. THAT WAS A RABBIT. DIDN'T YOU NOTICE HIS LONG FLOPPY EARS AND HIS FLUFFY TAIL? DID YOU SEE THE WAY HE HOPPED AWAY? RATS DON'T HOP LIKE THAT.
SOME DO!

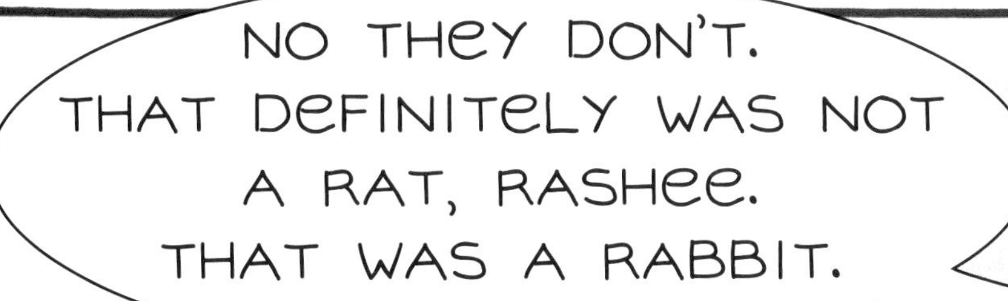
NO THEY DON'T. THAT DEFINITELY WAS NOT A RAT, RASHEE. THAT WAS A RABBIT.

ARE YOU SURE THAT WAS A RABBIT?
YES, I'M VERY SURE.

THE CLASS WALKED BY THE OLD TREES.

SOME OF THE TREES WERE
EVEN OLDER THAN THE SCHOOL!
MS. GWINN TOLD US TREES GIVE US
FRESH AIR TO BREATHE AND HELP
STOP GLOBAL WARMING.

MS. GWINN...

Oh my,
where?

THAT WASN'T A RAT BRIANNA. THAT WAS A SQUIRREL. DIDN'T YOU NOTICE HIS FURRY TAIL? DIDN'T YOU SEE THE WAY HE CLIMBED UP THE TREE AND JUMPED FROM BRANCH TO BRANCH? RATS DON'T JUMP LIKE THAT.
SOME DO!

NO... THAT WASN'T A RAT, BRIANNA. THAT WAS DEFINITELY A SQUIRREL.

ARE YOU SURE THAT WAS A SQUIRREL?
YES, VERY SURE.

NEXT, MS. GWINN LED US BY THE BARRELS USED TO CATCH THE RAIN.

MS. GWINN TOLD US THAT
WATER IS A PRECIOUS
RESOURCE AND SHOULD
NEVER BE WASTED.
BY PUTTING BARRELS
UNDER THE GUTTERS
WE COLLECT RAINWATER
OFF THE ROOF TO NOURISH OUR GARDEN.

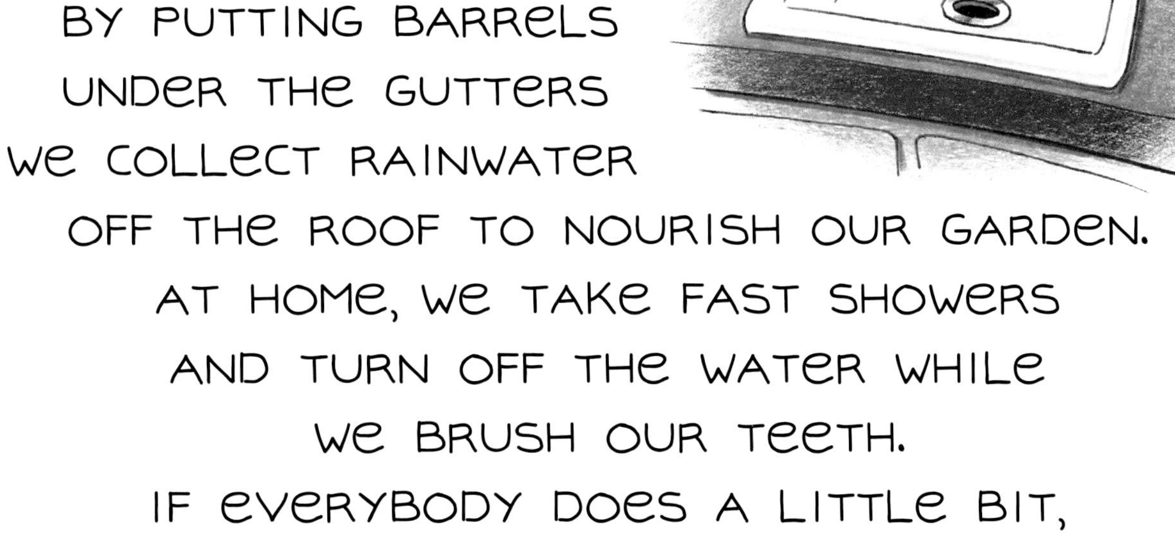

AT HOME, WE TAKE FAST SHOWERS
AND TURN OFF THE WATER WHILE
WE BRUSH OUR TEETH.
IF EVERYBODY DOES A LITTLE BIT,
WE CAN MAKE A BIG DIFFERENCE.

MS. GWINN...

THERE GOES A RAT!

Oh, puh-leez.

THAT'S NOT A RAT, DESMOND. THAT'S A CHIPMUNK. A DANDY LITTLE CHIPMUNK. DIDN'T YOU SEE HIS CUTE, STRIPED FACE AND HIS FLUFFY TAIL? RATS DON'T HAVE STRIPES LIKE THAT.

SOME DO!

RATS DON'T HAVE ANY HAIR ON THEIR TAILS AT ALL AND THEY SURELY AREN'T CUTE.
THAT DEFINITELY WAS NOT A RAT! THAT WAS A CHIPMUNK.

ARE YOU SURE THAT WAS A CHIPMUNK, MS GWINN?

YES, VERY SURE.

GLASS
PLASTIC
AFTER THAT WE WENT TO THE
RECYCLING AREA.

MS. GWINN TOLD US ***AGAIN***
ABOUT HOW IMPORTANT RECYCLING
IS TO PRESERVE OUR PLANET.
RECYCLING ALLOWS US TO REUSE
PLASTIC, PAPER AND GLASS PRODUCTS
TO SAVE OUR NATURAL RESOURCES.
DID YOU KNOW THAT PAPER COMES
FROM TREES AND PLASTIC IS
MADE FROM OIL?

MS. GWINN...

THERE GOES A RAT!

How may I help?

...AND THERE GOES MS. GWINN!
TEACHERS DON'T RUN LIKE THAT!
SOME DO!